★ THE ADVENTURES OF ★
TINTIN

THE ADVENTURES OF TINTIN: DANGER AT SEA
A BANTAM BOOK 978 0 857 51074 7

First published in the United States in 2011 by Little Brown

First published in Great Britain by Bantam,
an imprint of Random House Children's Books
A Random House Group Company

Bantam edition published 2011

1 3 5 7 9 10 8 6 4 2

Bantam Books are published by Random House Children's Books,
61–63 Uxbridge Road, London W5 5SA

www.kidsatrandomhouse.co.uk
www.totallyrandombooks.co.uk
www.randomhouse.co.uk

Addresses for companies within The Random House Group Limited can be found at: www.randomhouse.co.uk/offices.htm

THE RANDOM HOUSE GROUP Limited Reg. No. 954009

A CIP catalogue record for this book is available from the British Library.

Printed in Great Britain by Print 4 Limited.

★ THE ADVENTURES OF ★
TINTIN
DANGER AT SEA

Adapted by Kirsten Mayer

Screenplay by Steven Moffat

and Edgar Wright & Joe Cornish

Based on The Adventures of Tintin series by Hergé

BANTAM BOOKS

Attention, Tintin fans!
Can you find these items in this book?

SEAPLANE

MANUAL

PROPELLER

SAND DUNE

Tintin and his dog, Snowy,
like to find clues and solve crimes.
Sometimes they get into trouble
while trying to solve a mystery.

Tintin is on the trail of missing treasure!
So is Captain Haddock.
Tintin and the captain work together
to escape from the bad guys.

Tintin, Snowy and their new friend
have found more trouble!
They are in a small lifeboat
in the middle of the wide-open sea!

"We must go to the city of Bagghar," says Tintin.

"There we will find a clue to the treasure. Can you get us there, Captain?"

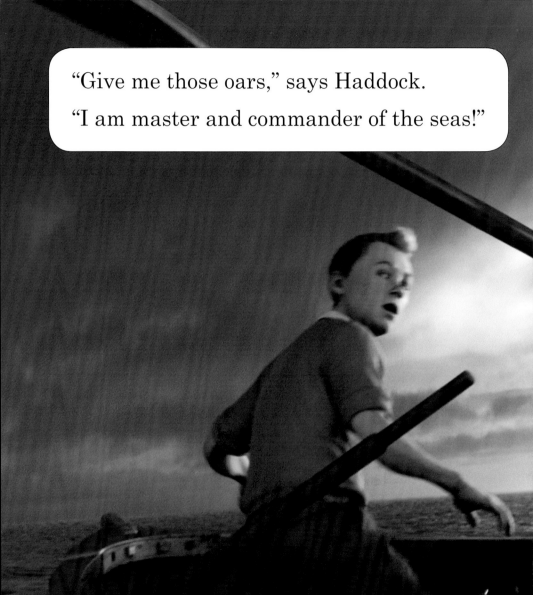

Haddock stands in the boat
to grab the oars from Tintin.
When he swings around,
the oars hit Tintin and Snowy!
He does not know that he has
knocked them out!

Haddock turns again.

"Look at the pair of them, fast asleep!

Never mind. I will get you there, Tintin."

The captain rows the boat for hours.

When Tintin wakes up,

he sees a fire inside the boat!

"Captain?" he asks. "What have you done?"

"You looked cold, so I lit a wee fire,"
explains Haddock.
"In a wooden boat?" cries Tintin.
Suddenly, the flames explode!

The three of them end up sitting
on top of the overturned boat.
"Well, this is a fine mess," says Tintin.
"Hopeless," agrees Haddock.

Snowy barks.

"What is it, Snowy?" asks Tintin.

He looks up. There is a seaplane!

Captain Haddock waves his arms.
"We are saved! We are saved!" he yells.
The plane banks towards the boat
and then begins to fire at them!
They are under attack!

"Captain, get down!" shouts Tintin.
Haddock jumps into the water
to hide behind the boat.

Tintin had saved a flare gun
from the lifeboat.
He fires the signal light,
and it hits the plane's engine.
"Well done, my boy!" cheers Haddock.

The seaplane's engine sputters out,
and the plane lands on the water.
They see two pilots climb out
and start fixing the engine.

"Wait here," says Tintin.

He swims over to the plane.

"Put your hands in the air!"

Tintin calls to the pilots in a bluff.

With the element of surprise,

Tintin and Haddock take care of the pilots.

But who will fly the plane?

Tintin looks through the manual.

"You do know what you are doing, right?"
asks Haddock.

"More or less," answers Tintin.

"Well, which is it? More or less?"

Tintin gets the plane in the air.

"We are off to Bagghar!" he says.

Haddock is still worried.

"Is there another way," he asks,

"that does not take us into that storm?"

There are big black clouds ahead.

Snowy barks. They fly right into them!

Lightning flashes.

"The fuel tank is almost empty," says Tintin.
"Captain, climb out of the plane
and pour fuel into the tank!"
"Christopher Columbus!" cries Haddock.
"There is a storm out there!"

"We are running on fumes!" yells Tintin.
Captain Haddock goes out of the door
and manages to pour fuel into the tank.
The plane propeller spins again.
"Captain, it is working!" cries Tintin.

But Haddock sees something.

"Land! Land!" he shouts.

"We are not there yet," replies Tintin.

Then he sees it, too: a huge sand dune!

Tintin manages to miss the dune,
but there are more ahead.
They are going to crash!
"Hang on!" cries Haddock.
The plane smashes into the sand,
but they are okay!

The three friends set off across the sand on their next adventure.

"We have to keep going!" says Tintin.

"On to Bagghar and to the treasure!"